Tir's Trial

A Fantasy Short Story
By Alfred Muller

Enjoy the journey !!

Dedication

This short story is dedicated to all the great fantasy writers who inspired me to try my hand at story telling.

Copyright © 2022 Alfred Muller All rights reserved

The characters and events portrayed in this book are fictitious. Any similarity to real persons, living or dead, is coincidental and not intended by the author.

No part of this book may be reproduced, or stored in a retrieval system, or transmitted in any form or by any means, electronic, mechanical, photocopying, recording, or otherwise, without express written permission of the publisher.

Cover design by: Nicole Honl
Printed in the United States of America

Table of Contents

Tir's Trial	1
Dedication	2
Copyright	3
Drip….	6
Author's Note	42
Look for me	45

Drip... drip... drip, drip. Water drops fell from the leaves in the canopy above Tir's head. A full day into his trial it finally ceased its barrage of droplets. Clouds drifted lazily parting here and there stretching a tattered grey blanket across the sky. Lush greens and vibrant yellows polka-dotted the trees in the forest as the change of seasons began. As Tir rested his back against a damp tree his vest soaked up the moisture. Shifting to get comfortable, his back slid over the bumpy trunk scraping off loose bark. The fresh under-bark gave off a mossy smell.

A snapping twig brought Tir's blue eyes open. He had been alone so far. Not even a squirrel crossed his path. With the stories told of these woods, from his village elders in his mind, Tir held his breath.

Leaves ruffled closer on his right side. He slowly lifted himself off the ground gripping the two protruding roots at his sides to do so. Using every muscle Tir controlled his movements meticulously placing his feet on clearly visible dirt. Slowly, he turned to his left. Hugging the tree Tir peered around it. A couple yards away stood a bandit with a repeating crossbow.

A pulley system, attached to a spring, drew back the string after the small weapon was fired while another arrow rose from a compartment below. What should have been bright Oakwood was dark stained from the heavy rain. The added weight would cause it to function less than perfect, Tir hoped.

Thank Odin for nature's changing seasons. Tir thought to himself observing the bandit.

A dark piece of cloth covered the bandit's face below his eyes. Black hair fell over the bandit's forehead and ears overlapping with the cloth leaving only their eyes exposed. The physique, thin with long limbs and a small chest made it hard to discern male from female. Pale skin peaked out at the bandit's wrists between his long sleeves and gloves. They wore thick pants to protect their legs. This bandit's pants lay in dark wrinkles by their boots.

Wiping small beads of sweat from their eyes, the bandit continued on his or her way. Tir slowly moved around the tree keeping it between him and the bandit. Tir's sole focus was seized by dumb luck. The leather sole of Tir's boot did well against rocks and sticks, but was little use on a slick tree root. His leg flew out from under him sending him crashing into a pile of leaves and twigs. The bandit whirled around at the noise, firing instinctively. The bolt hit the tree where Tir was hiding.

Tir clawed his way to his feet. He ignored the uncomfortable sensation of mud under his nails as another bolt whizzed by his ear. His dash from danger could be viewed as comical. He slid across water logged leaves, tripped over hidden roots all while attempting to gain traction on the muddy forest floor. Numerous times he wondered how he was still alive.

Tir's thighs were rubbed raw from the fabric of his slacks. Sweat continued to lubricate the fabric keeping the discomfort fresh in his mind. In this area of the forest bushes were sparse. Most of the space between tall trees was empty except for flying bolts. One cut across the air tearing at Tir's skin. He knew he was cut, but the pain hadn't registered yet. While he wasn't out of breath, he wasn't built for long distance running either. It was impossible to tell how many bolts had been let loosed. Unless the bandit ran out Tir was in trouble.

Tir thought back to a story from his village that might help. A group of bandits once tracked and treed one of his people's greatest warriors. For three days they fired bolts at him from the ground. The warrior hid amongst the leaves and branches until dark. While Tir's people were much stockier than the nimble bandits they were at home in the woods. He leapt to an adjacent tree and shimmied down. The bandits unaware of their prey's actions continued to fire at the empty tree top. He easily dispatched the bandits once their ammunition ran out.

Tir wasn't sure he had the time to wait for this bandit's quiver to run dry, but perhaps he could use the wilderness to his advantage just like the warrior. Two bolts flew passed Tir burring themselves in the ground. One of them had more of Tir's fresh blood on its tip.

Ahead the ground split where an old river may have once run. If nothing else it may provide some cover from the bolts. It could also trap Tir in a hole in the ground. Jumping into the small gully Tir heard the wiz of a bolt overhead. It flew through the air where his head had been seconds earlier.

The bandit skidded to a stop over the break in the earth. Puddles seeped from the saturated ground along the old creek bed. Muddy walls rose up around them revealing roots of nearby trees. Ripples danced across the water surfaces masking which way the boy may have gone. A section of mud gave way splashing down into a puddle covering it with black earth. Leaning over the edge, he gazed one way, then the next, but he saw nothing. The ground gave way a little and the bandit stepped away from the edge. Satisfied that the boy had continued running, the bandit loaded a few more bolts and followed the gully on the left.

After a brief period of quiet waiting, the bandit's pounding feet were out of earshot. Peeling himself away from the mud and grime of the wall Tir ran. His hair was covered with mud swaying back and forth as he ran. His pace had slowed now fighting the suction of the mud as he ran. The cut in his leg brush gritty dirt with each step. After trudging through mud, almost losing his boots twice, Tir finally saw an incline that lead to sturdier ground.

The gully thinned until it was barely shoulder width. As the ground rose it also became more solid. Tir bounced off both walls of the gully fighting to keep his balance. More sun rays pierced the shield of leaves above. It warmed his skin giving him a boost of energy enough to propel him out of the gully. Tir heard splashing footsteps to his left. While the sun felt good its presence created a thin fog. At a distance it was hard to see what made the noise. A drone of a dozen others followed. They seemed to come from everywhere. The canopy echoed the splashes back to the forest floor. The footsteps grew louder until Tir saw the bandit run past. Growls and bays made up the howl of a pack of wolves. They nipped at the bandit's ankles keeping pace with their two-legged prey.

Two wolves caught up to him. Running alongside they steered the bandit where they wanted him to go. Trapped, and too close to use his crossbow, the bandit leaped at a tree. Pushing off it with one leg he spun and shot the wolf on his left with a bolt.

Tir's eyes narrowed. The bandit had changed direction, heading back towards him. Glancing around he searched for a stick, a rock, anything he could use as a weapon. Most of the sticks on the floor had wood rot and would be too fragile to make a useful club.

The pack had closed in and Tir still could not find a weapon. The bandit tried his trick again but a third wolf leaped from the brush, clamping its jaws around the bandit's arm holding the crossbow.

"Get off of me, you damn feral mutt," the bandit yelled as he hit the ground, more than arm's length away from his crossbow. The other wolves converged on the bandit uncaring of his screams.

Tir knew he should have run. One skinny bandit wouldn't sustain the pack for long. Passing on the opportunity to grab a weapon, however could be worse. Other creatures, more dangerous than a pack of wolves, lurked in the woods. Heart pounding in his chest Tir wiped his muddy hands against the mud of his vest. His muscles fought against his common sense, as he slowly and cautiously walked up to the feeding pack. As his arm stretched out, streaked were sweat had parted the grim, a growl stopped him. A large male stood two feet away its teeth bared in its bloody maw.

"Easy boy, I need this." Tir kept eye contact with the wolf. Any movement could set it off, but he'd come this far and he needed that weapon. "That's it, I'm not an enemy."

The wolf barked a warning.

Once the bow was in Tir's hand, he backed away his free hand in the air continuing eye contact. In a twist of luck both the wolf and Tir looked away at the same time.

His back to the pack of wolves Tir walked away. The buildup of anticipation urging him to run. Hunting parties always returned with stories about wolf packs. The two groups battled for superiority out here. Occasionally they faced off. The loser the one to show weakness first. Tir forced himself to walk as he strained to hear any running behind him.

Once safely away from the pack, Tir's nerves settled. The hair on the back of his neck relaxed. His shoulders slouched. He limped when he walked resisting putting pressure on his injured leg. A brutal sting pulsated up his dominant arm so he carried the crossbow awkwardly in the other. Tir paused to access his injuries. He leaned the crossbow against a tree surveying his arm first. Twisting it to get a better look the skin slipped from his grip smearing mud over the wound. Tir winced. Grinding his teeth against the pain he punched the nearest tree. The shock dropped a hand full of water on his head.

Shivering through the freezing bath he turned to his leg next. Red skin puffed up around the edges of the wound. Tir was no herb grinder, but he understood that wasn't good. This section of forest didn't provide much in the way of cover. Scattered saplings and thorn bushes mingled above flat terrain. Tall trees' branches protruded more than two of Tir's six feet overhead. He would have to plunge deeper into the woods if he wanted anything suitable for shelter. It had not been his plan to wander far from his village. Five miles at most. After his chase with the bandit he sat near eight miles. Any farther and he would be in the Wild Wood. Tales of its nightmarish inhabitants haunted nighttime fires. He needed to get dry and care for his wounds.

A large tree lay between the fork of two trunks of another three. The larger tree's branches were bare of leaves, but the density of branches provided adequate cover. The natural formation reminded Tir of makeshift homes his people had made by leaning cut branches against a fallen tree. Moss fell away under his grip as he eased himself under the larger trees cover. Small saplings sprouted from the fallen trees stump. The recent storm wasn't the reason it lay down now.

Tir grabbed a nearby leaf with some water on it to pour over his leg. It stung, but it needed cleaning. He looked around for more leaves and found none. His arm needed attention too. He was taught that the bandits who frequented the woods used serrated arrows usually laced with poison. From the odd angle of the wound on his arm it was hard to tell how bad it was. He saw the torn flesh and ripped meat of his leg, assuming his arm must look similar. It didn't burn like his leg did. He concluded he had been hit with one poisoned arrow and one mundane arrow. Lucky him. The hair around the wound was covered in dried blood and his skin was wrinkled. Under the canopy of trees was dry which he needed. Out there amongst the living plants were useful plants he could make salves out of which he needed more. Tir took up the crossbow. Its string was released and all the slots for extra bolts were empty. Cursing, he tossed it away. It clanked, bouncing hard off the sopping ground. If a bolt remained it may have held a clue as to what poison infected him and he still needed a weapon. Grunting as the cut in his leg stretched, he stood and limped into the trees.

The only way to survive the forest his father told him was to face the dangerous areas. He now believed like many of the other men from his village who passed their trial that he was exaggerating. Rays played on the back of Tir's neck. He guessed at the height of the sun that he had about five hours of daylight left. He searched all around his dry shelter before abandoning it for better prospects. He really did not want to enter the Wild Wood in his condition. That was the purpose of these trials though. To test ones, resolve in harsh conditions. In spite of his trepidation he crossed the boundary into the fabled wood. At least what he thought was the boundary. There was no hard line drawn simply a vague understanding of the area where the two sections met. He did find some prospective herbs that he believed to be useful, but by the time he checked the amount of daylight he'd become lost. If he was allowed a knife on his trial, he would have marked trees. Too many stories were told of those who wandered into the Wild Wood becoming lost as the living trees moved to alter the terrain. Tir spent the remainder of daylight heading back the way he came. After the sun set, he continued to look for the shelter he had abandoned more so for bearing than shelter. He didn't stop until his leg hurt up to his thigh. By then he was drenched in sweat and exhausted. He sat down by a small tree.

It wasn't sleep that took him. It was similar. He was unconscious. A fire had been lit in his wound. His body reacted to the pain by causing his leg to twitch. That only opened the wound more allowing the poison to seep deeper into his body. He was unaware of the two predators sneaking through the woods following his scent.

* * *

The two creatures looked elf like with pale skin and pointed ears. Their nimbleness as they avoided the plants and vegetation struck true as an elf as well. In many ways' elf could be used to describe these creatures, but for their allergy to sunlight. A fermenting aroma of yeast followed them as they stalked the young one lying unconscious.

Ivelk in the elven tongue or Tainted One in the language most spoke is what they were known as. The true elf who stalked the predators didn't care for terminology. He simply wanted to prevent them from spreading their taint. He caught up to them as one held the unconscious human in its arms. Two perfectly-aimed fangs punctured the boy's neck. Blood poured into the Ivelk's mouth as an arrow pierced its heart. The elf leapt into the clearing before the arrow had time to fall to the ground. Dust filled the area coating the grass, the boy, the elf, and the remaining Ivelk. Nature could not abide an abomination such as the Ivelk to exist, yet they did. Their existence was strenuous at best. They were easy to kill if you could match them in speed and dexterity. A slight distortion to their heart area removed them from existence. The elf didn't draw back on his bow to kill the second one. He plucked the still falling arrow from the air driving the arrow tip into its chest.

The elf knelt down beside the boy checking him over. Blood dribbled from the thorn sized holes in his neck. Other than the bite the boy had a flesh wound reopened on the back side of his arm and a gash on his leg that appeared poisoned. It was a miracle the boy was still alive. The elf tended to the unconscious boy caring for his arm and cleaning his leg wound after arranging a quick campsite. He forced broth down his throat to help counter act the poison in his leg. Had the poisoned arrow hit his arm it may have already reached his heart. This human child was lucky. Shadows stretched along the forest floor. The barest hint of stars twinkled into existence in the darkening sky as the boy slept.

* * *

Tir was uncomfortable. His arm was stiff. He couldn't use it to bat away the coals burning on his neck. At times he thought he was dreaming. He couldn't remember entering the luscious section of forest where bright trees surrounded him, grass cushioned his feet and everything smelled of sugar.

Voices spoke from all around him. Some of the words were in a different language, but all had a relaxing tone like the coo of a mother.

"Trespass."
"Human."
"Do not belong."
"Flee."

Out of the trees, the ground, the air creatures made of that material appeared. Their skin glowed from a single light, in the center of their transparent chest. Some were blue, others green, the one that rose from the ground was a very light brown. All of them surrounded Tir repeating the same few sentences. Tir recognized these forest creatures from fire side stories. They live in service of nature. They do not like humans. And... And... there was another aspect of their nature that seemed important, but the thought would not formulate for him. He also could not remember the names of these creatures. All of them crossed their arms over their chests scowling as they surrounded him. Tir knew that he was in trouble. Fear clarified one thing for him. The thought he couldn't remember flared bright as the pain in his neck. These creatures enter the dreams of humans, driving them mad.

"Get out of my head!"

"Not fun, when unwanted are in your space," one said, and the rest echoed the last two words.

"You don't own the forest, but this is my head," Tir said turning this way and that trying to escape, but the creatures surrounded him.

"Child, this is our mind, body, and life," one snapped.

"And life," others repeated.

"Without a forest we do not exist."

"You drive men insane. Even some of the strongest of warriors, but I am not afraid," Tir said finding it hard to believe his own words. He glanced around for a weapon and found nothing he could use. The creatures closed in on him.

"Fear."

"Fear."

"You fear."

"Us." The last to speak glowed green. It smiled at him. She was beautiful. Her hair shined like sun baked meadows. Her translucent skin was fluorescent, smooth as silk. Vines draped over her body and leaves covered her in appropriate areas while still leaving most of her body exposed. Even in his dreams he flushed and looked away. Her voice spoke to Tir's spirit, entering his ears washing through him like a waterfall over rocks.

She crept in real close. She raised his head. He could only see her face.

"You are mine now son of man," she said, moving her lips slow, getting closer to Tir's. Their lips touched she kissed Tir. Her hands held him in place. Green veins rose on Tir's face starting at his lips extending to his ears. The veins curled around his temple. As quick as it began the creature broke the kiss and pulled away. She shrieked in pain. Tir woke up.

Tir swung his arms and wiped at his mouth in the sudden fit of consciousness. Once he realized he was awake his hands shot to his face. He ran his hands along his squared jaw, up his smooth face to his temple and then to the fire at his neck. Two bumps were raised under his touch. "Where am I," he asked to no one.

"Safe."

Tir spun toward the voice noticing the elf for the first time. The elf's hair was long and black, falling down past his chest in pin straight lines. His nose looked human, a little elongated and slim, but human.

There was no hair on his arm or face. His skin was the color of burnt wood, as if he spent most of his time in the sun. His eyes were dark grey and flat as his expression.

"I am Aelsun. I've treated your wounds, dosed you with an antitoxin for the poison in your leg, and kept you from dying. Your welcome. Perhaps you could explain what you are doing in these woods. I thought humans knew to avoid this area."

The elf's grasp of his language was startling. He had never met one before. His people only knew of them through stories passed down through generations. He didn't know some still existed let alone lived so close to his village.

"I'm in the middle of my trial."

"Are you guilty of some crime?"

"No. All of my people go through it. Only those who survive for a time in the woods are allowed to come back to the village."

"Too bad. I'd hoped you were exiled."

"That's odd. You saved my life?" Tir's anger was subverted by the grumble that roared in his stomach.

"I meant no offense by it. Please eat, I've made stew. Eat and we will talk. It might lighten the news I must share with you."

Tir was hesitant to take the wooden bowl from Aelsun. He was alive. His life spared. Perhaps it was about his leg? Maybe the antitoxin was administered too late and he was to lose his leg? Tir ran a hand along the wound there. It no longer burned under his touch. White linen or fabric weaved between the split pulling the wound closed. Tir had never seen such a thing. As he rubbed at it, he felt a tug on his arm where the other arrow had hit him.

"What is this?"

"Those are fibers from a tree. I harvested them myself. They come in handy for large wounds like yours. You like the stew?"

Aelsun looked to be forty. Lines streaked across his forehead and bags hung under his eyes. Any youthful glow had vanished from his demeanor ages ago. He wore green cloth that clung tight to his thin physique. He wasn't scrawny. Tir could see the definition in his muscle as he moved about checking the stew and fiddling with spices in pouches around his waist. His shirt was long-sleeved probably to protect his arms from his bow which currently lay slung on his back. His clothes were a little thread bare and looked as if they could use a cleaning. His pants were the same fabric as Tir's. The elf's pants were camouflaged to the bark on the trees surrounding them.

"Stews good. Thank you."

"How are you feeling?"

"Slight pain in my neck and my leg is a little itchy where the fibers are. I appreciate what you did for me."

Aelsun finished off his bowl of stew and set it aside. "Have you ever heard of Ivelk?"

"I don't understand that word."

"Here," Aelsun said pouring more stew into Tir's bowl. "Ivelk are abominations. Their sole purpose is to spread their disease and corrupt nature. They normally avoid areas of dense forest because they are highly sensitive to it. One prick from a thorn or slash from a branch will kill them. Two of them were attacking you when I found you."

Tir's hand went to his neck and the two bumps. "Why were they out here then?"

"That is what I aim to find out. Normally they stick to caves or the occasional town. They burn down sections of woods and poison the minds of men who do their bidding for them. Ivelk are an infection much like the poison in your leg. Unfortunately, they have no cure."

"Am I infected?"

"That is a loaded question. Before I found you one of them was feeding off of your blood. It is how they survive. Once an Ivelk feeds the victim contracts their disease. Had I not been hunting them and they decided to feed you some of their own blood you would be infected. Because you did not feed from them you are simply bonded to that Ivelk."

"But you said you killed them."

"Precisely. This leaves you in a hopeless situation."

"Am I going to die?"

"No, but you may wish you were. Because the Ivelk who drank from you is dead you will gradually become lonely. Even if you have a large family with dozens of children and grandchildren the incompleteness you feel will only grow."

"I wish you would have let me die."

"I've done that before. It was a mistake then and it would have been a mistake now." Aelsun spoke from years of contemplating a decision that completely changed his life. The weight behind his words wasn't lost on Tir who did not argue the point. He didn't feel any different yet. Perhaps the elf was wrong. Perhaps the Ivelk hadn't drank too much.

"Tell me more of this trial. Are you to kill a legendary beast? Pluck a pedal from one of the sapient plants with in the Sentient Wood?"

Tir had no desire to talk, but Aelsun had been good to him so he felt obligated. "Nothing as grand as that, however it doesn't hurt to come back with tales of heroic feats. The trial requires on your thirteenth year to set out unarmed into the wilderness. You must survive for three days. If you arrive back at the village before then you are exiled. If you do not come back after ten days you are mourned, but eventually forgotten about."

"Seems barbaric even for humans. You aren't given weapons or supplies?" Aelsun said cleaning up his cook pot and bowls.

"It is how my people have survived in the woods for so long. We try to stay clear of, what did you call it? Sentient? We call these woods, Wild Woods. I came this way looking for food. I must learn to provide for myself before I can provide for my village." Tir set his bowl aside gesturing he was full as Aelsun offered more food. "My people have a saying. A village can only survive if everyone is strong. If someone isn't providing their own share of work than someone else has to take up the slack. I don't expect you to understand, but it is our way."

"My people once held ceremonial practices like those of which you speak. They were outlawed some time ago. They were brutal. Part combat, part intellect. Problem solving and the like." Aelsun waved his hand as if to forget the memory then changed the subject. "You've been sleeping for two days since I found you. How long have you been out here?"

"That makes four. It was my second day when I wondered into the Wild Wood. I guess I can go home now."

"Not exactly. We have other problems," Aelsun said, rolling up the blanket he was sitting on.

"Are their more Ivelk?"

"They are not the threat anymore. Please," Aelsun gestured to the blanket Tir was sitting on. He stood and Aelsun rolled that up too.

"Are we not staying here for the night?"

"It's not safe. Everywhere Ivelk go a pack of Wraiths follow. But I promise if we survive the night, I'll make sure you get to your village," Aelsun said.

Tir had heard of Wraiths before. He wasn't sure if they were the same thing that Aelsun was talking about or not. Tir's understanding of the creatures was vague. When a warrior died in an unsatisfactory way their spirit would haunt the world seeking for absolution. Aelsun moved about dousing the fire, kicking around the ground, masking their presence. Tir was less certain Aelsun meant the same creature. Tir's Wraith didn't track its adversaries. They came ambushed those unfortunate enough to stumble upon their graves. Tir did his best to help, but his arm was still sore and he moved delicately on his wounded leg. Once their camp site looked more or less how Aelsun found it he led Tir into the Sentient woods.

"I don't think Wraith means the same thing in my language as it does in yours. Why did we kick up the camp?"

"Wraiths are Wraiths. It's an old custom of my people. Return things to how they were when you leave. While some tales may be skewed to fit each people's beliefs, Wraiths are lost spirits at the bare bones of their being. Wraiths in my context are spirits driven from the body after an Ivelk has turned their victim."

"I couldn't bare being a wandering spirit."

Trees with wide trunks sprouted up from the forest floor. Tir knew he was being watched. Everything appeared normal then movement from the corner of his vision made him second guess his assumption. For the first time he began to worry whether the elf was helping him or leading him to a trap. The realization came to late however. They were half a day's run into the Wild Wood. If the stories were true the landscape in here could change as you passed erasing any signs you'd been there. So, Tir followed Aelsun who constantly checked to make sure he wasn't outpacing the injured human. Aelsun was everything Tir imagined an elf would be. Lithe and quick, he never mis-stepped. The woods seemed to mold around him. He hoped Aelsun was an ally because he was afraid to see him in a fight.

"Why do Wraiths follow Ivelk?"

"Wraiths follow the Ivelk that turn them. It's believed they try to kill that Ivelk to set themselves free. They never tire. They are always hunting. They are especially dangerous for the survivors of attacks. Any unfortunate enough to live through an Ivelk attack and who has been bitten may have their life drained by a Wraith."

"You aren't reassuring me any."

Aelsun stopped and put a hand on Tir's chest. "I'm not trying to reassure you. Out here truth leads to survival. Hiding things only gets you killed. You will have to run for the rest of your life if we do not destroy the Wraiths chasing you. Because I don't know how many there are, I am trying to find a defensible position. Then I will tell you where to go to get back to your village."

"I'm not going to help you fight? I'm a good warrior. What if they kill you and then come find me while I'm at my village? They'll kill everyone there. I'm not going back until I know it's safe."

"You understand it may take more than ten days to dispatch them."

Tir had not thought of that. "Why so long? Can't we just ambush them?" A few heroic tales Tir grew up with told of warriors with weapons of magic that could kill anything. One such tale was of a brave warrior who entered a graveyard disturbing dozens of Wraiths. He drew his sword and cut them all down. It was a tale, but there should be some truth to it.

"No, we cannot. Wraiths aren't physical beings like us. They are specters. They require special weapons to kill. Even then it is dubious at best. If you are going to kill any Wraith, one two, twenty you need the proper placement."

Tir looked expectantly.

"There needs to be running water near a Hawthorn Tree. This is common in the Sentient Wood, but we aren't near a river and the closest Hawthorn is two days run. Three with your injured leg. That brings you to seven days. Do you see the problem?"

"That would leave me with three days to get back before I was exiled."

Aelsun nodded. "If you insist on fighting, follow me for now and make a final decision when we find the proper environment."

Tir nodded.

"Very well. Let's see how far that leg can get you."

***

That night and the next Aelsun kept watch asking Tir to only keep guard for four hours. Two hours at dusk after Aelsun reapplied a poultice to Tir's leg and two hours at dawn before they struck out. During those two-hour intervals Aelsun slept. During the day they ran. Tir found strength in his leg after the first night. Whatever Aelsun had done seemed to work quick. They thought they may have found a Hawthorn on the second day since they left the original campsite, but it was only an Alder tree.

"Do we head up river and hope there is one up there or keep going to where I know there is one."

"Why are you asking me?"

"What are you willing to risk? It is possible there is a Hawthorn up river I do not know about and you may be able to stay until the fight is over. By my judgment if we find a tree up river the Wraiths will be on us tonight. If we continue through today and some of the night, we should face the Wraiths by dusk tomorrow."

"I'd rather stick to what you know. This forest makes me feel like prey."

"Keep that feeling. It will help you survive."

As they ran on towards the Hawthorn Tree Tir saw things he'd never imagined. Plant stalks tall as trees with large red bulbs moving about in the breezeless canopy. Small roots reaching out beneath underbrush and bushes trying to grab at his legs. Leaves moving across their path, vines lowering themselves in hopes to grab a snack, a deer trapped in the mouth of a large green and red plant. Tir almost ran into a large spiked bulb that launched itself from behind a copse of trees. Aelsun had to pull him back, saving his life again.

"Pay attention or you will die out here."

"How long have you lived out here?"

"Too long. Now come on?"

Tir was exhausted when they set up camp near midnight. They ate cold bread and hard cheese. Tir couldn't have hoped for better company during his trial. He couldn't enjoy it though. The loneliness Aelsun had warned him about started to fill his heart. Aelsun described to Tir the various living-thinking plants throughout the Sentient Wood and Tir felt as if he'd ignored him the entire time. He heard the words, but it was as if they didn't stick. He was present with Aelsun and yet he wasn't. Tir felt more alone now than he had during the first few days of his trial.

"What's it like being exiled?" Tir said unable to overcome the depression that weighed on him. He didn't think he would make it home in time.

"What do you mean?" Aelsun said. He held a blade of grass in his slender hands. He weaved it between nimble fingers, nicking the ends with pointed nails. He was forming some kind of basket, but the object was too small for Tir to see clearly.

"I figured you lived out here because you were exiled."

"Not a bad guess I suppose, but I wasn't exiled. I left willingly,"

"You can do that?"

"It's a long story and you need to get some sleep. Let's just say my kind and I haven't seen eye to eye for a long time," Aelsun said.

They settled into a companionable silence which suited Aelsun fine, but only highlighted Tir's growing loneliness.

"If we kill these Wraiths, will this sickness in my stomach go away?"

Aelsun finished fiddling with the blade of grass and tossed it to Tir. "I'm sorry, but no. It will subside some I suppose, but over the course of your life it will continue to gnaw at you. Every friendship you make will be tainted with it. Every relationship you have now will not feel the same. It is a great burden you live with."

Tir moved the small weaved item in his hand. It wasn't a basket, but a sphere made from a single blade of grass. The weaved pattern allowed for tiny holes to see through. At its center was a tiny spark.

"What's this?"

"A bit of elven magic. A lost art amongst my people. It has no real purpose except to inspire hope. Anytime you feel down remember me, a friend.

Someone who helped you out of this predicament. Maybe it will help."

"I don't mean to be rude, but the stories I've heard of elves don't paint them in a fine light." Aelsun nodded as Tir continued. "Why help me, a human?"

"My people have fallen far from our former glory. The ruling council believes we should hide away for our past crimes. I think we should go back out into the world and make amends for what we've done. I like to think I am doing a small part in that by helping you."

Tir was overwhelmed with emotion. Between the battling depression inside him and the heaping care from Aelsun, Tir couldn't speak. The tiny glow inside the blade of grass shone a little brighter Tir thought. After a time Aelsun rolled over to sleep when he noticed Tir rubbing at his neck.

"How's that bite?"

"Throbbing, why?"

"I was afraid of that." Aelsun's expression darkened.

"What does that mean," Tir asked, looking around. The air around the dark campsite dropped in temperature. Bumps rose over his arms. He rubbed at them to little effect.

"Wraiths," Aelsun said. "Get up. We have to go."

"Go, but we just stopped. Can't we fight them here?"

"If your desire is to die than yes. If you wish to live to see your village again you will get up and run."

A hollow howl cut through the night raising the hair companions' necks. Flickering grey silhouettes hovered from the depth of the forest. Tir and Aelsun focused their attention ahead of them, fully aware of the cold presence closing in behind them. Running in the Sentient Woods was daring on the clearest, brightest noon day. At night it was near suicide. The equivalent could be said about waiting for a pack of Wraiths.

"How much farther do we have?"

Aelsun's response was to fire an arrow at the nearest Wraith. The arrowhead produced a dull blue glow. Not unlike that of the moon. At full draw, Tir thought the bow would snap or the string would break. Its tension seemed not to phase the elf, who scanned the tree line for his target.

"Keep going until you hear the sound of running water. Once you reach the river submerge yourself waist deep."

"Then what?"

"Wait for me."

"I don't understand."

Aelsun let another arrow fly piercing the closest Wraith in the chest. The arrow seemed to pass through harmlessly, but a second later the Wraith vaporized. "You don't need to. Just run," Aelsun said, then as an afterthought said, "Wait. Take this too."

The elf grabbed his dagger and handed it to Tir. Tir grasp the hilt which held a blade as long as his forearm. The grip, a perfect fit in Tir's hand, was cold to the touch, but not so cold as to inflict pain. The dagger grew heavier at the tip forcing itself down before losing all weight and rising up again. He was exhausted. All of Tir's aches from the hard traveling stopped when he grabbed the hilt. He was refreshed, renewed. He could run another hundred miles if he needed.

"Those arrows are killing them. Can't I stay and help?"

Aelsun spun on Tir and pushed him up stream towards the Hawthorne. "Go!"

Tir stumbled before catching himself falling into a steady jog. Reluctant to leave him, Tir did as he was told. He barreled through the woods using the blue glow from the dagger to light his way. His leg muscles were tight including his wounded leg which gave out every several steps or so. He gained small cuts from thorns and twigs that lashed out as he ran. Sweat dripped into the wounds stinging as it mingled with fresh blood. A choir of howls pierced the night. Aelsun winced and Tir fought the reflex to grab his ears.

Aelsun was the one who said they needed the river and Hawthorn to face the Wraiths, yet he was staying behind to fight. How was he going to stand against them? It made no sense. Even if he found a way to stall them long enough for Tir to get to the river, how was he going to out run them? Unless he was holding back. How fast could the elf actually move? For a moment Tir debated entering the river and travelling up stream in the water. He decided against it, the water would slow him down. Instead he turned away from the water heading for a less overgrown path. He hoped the level ground would make it easier on his leg.

The slightest moment of split focus cost Tir. Finger-like roots spread out in front of him attempting to trip him up. At first it felt as if his foot caught on a rock or something in the darkness. Then it happened again and again. He fought to keep his balance. Each time his feet came down another of these roots snatched at him until he could stay up no longer. He hit the ground jarring his injured arm. Dozens of finger-like roots scurried over him, gripping his arms and legs, snatching at his clothes, pulling on his hair. The dagger flew from his grasp and was immediately snatched up by one of the little roots. Tir struggled against his bonds. They pulled him in all directions. At first it was similar to a child tugging on his arm. It wasn't a gradual growth from that to a horse taking off with his arm stuck in its reins. How his arm remained attached he wasn't sure. Tir looked up to see the roots that clung to the dagger recoil in pain.

So, it wasn't just good for Wraiths. The blade hurt whatever these things were. If he could pull his arms free. Everything was easier when it was in his head. He thought his trial would be easy. He thought he'd hang around and enter his village on the third day. He thought he could just pull his arm free. None of that happened. Instead the roots pulled on him. His injured leg screamed as roots gripped the torn skin and pulled. One scurried over his mouth and pulled on his cheek. Tir did the only thing he could --- he bit. He bit down hard. A sweet tangy liquid dripped into his mouth and the end of the root he severed stopped writhing. A handful of roots pulled away freeing his injured arm. His feet were still restrained, but he lunged with all he had scratching at the ground to gather up the dagger.

"Abomination! You insist on disrupting nature. Predator-and-prey is as natural as the sun. It's simply less fun when you are the prey. Stop struggling. Let the Grippers have you."

"Call them off of me."

"Unlike you, I allow the natural order to complete its course." The green creature from his dream shimmered into existence. Her flawless complexion was ruined by a black burn across her face and lips. She held up her hand and a sapling sprouted from the ground. Thin branches peeled away unfurling tiny green leaves. She spun her hand and the sapling grew in girth. Wrinkles formed on the once smooth trunk. Its dark brown muted to dull grey and then black as the tree collapsed and decayed. In the matter of moments Tir witnessed the birth and death of a tree. What power this creature had. "You are a vial taint to nature. You've infected me and for that you will die."

"Get them off of me," Tir said again. Begging would seem a viable option at this point for Tir, but it never entered his mind. To beg would be to show weakness. To show weakness would invite others to look at him as prey. In spite of his truly dire predicament Tir chose anger instead.

"Poor naive child. You are dense as you are witless. I have not commanded these grippers to attack you. You provoked them by being here. I simply will not stop them."

Tir felt burning in his muscles and tendons as the remaining grippers pulled on his body. He stretched again and again for the dagger, but could not reach it. Suddenly the temperature dropped. Bumps prickled up his arms and legs.

"I could have made you great. Shown you nature in its truest form. Instead you taint it with your every breath. You will die and I will watch. You will hear my laughter as your soul is dragged from you. And once they are finished, I will make sure my pets feed on your corpse."

Tir struggled more half listening to the forest spirit. "I am going to find the tree, where you dwell, and burn it down," Tir promised. The effect was less than he hoped as he gasped for breath between each word.

"You will never live to find it," the green woman said dismissively.

"Then I will spend my afterlife corrupting the entire forest," Tir growled. He managed enough breath to make the threat seem possible.

She balked at the threat, meaningless to her. Her mind already on other plans she turned away and faded into the dark forest.

Tir cared little if she was here or not. He tore at the roots clinging to his other arm. His fingers on that arms began to tingle under the root's pressure. Without another option he twisted his torso until his mouth could reach the root and bit down. The earthy taste rolled around his mouth until the tangy liquid burst across his tongue. Another few roots retreated freeing his non-injured leg. While he couldn't contort his body enough to bend and bite the last root, there was enough slack to reach the dagger now. In a blink Tir snatched it up and severed the root. He got to his feet gingerly. Relieved to be free he shook out his arm hoping to get feeling back.

Freezing breath stung like winter's wind on the back of his neck. An apparition flickered into existence in front of Tir. Its face a screaming mask of shadow. If there had ever been facial features they were lost to darkness. Its body was nearly translucent, only the hint of grey haze giving it form. He swiped at it with the dagger but it vanished before the blade touched it. With the path open Tir ran. It was more of a hobbling trot. He couldn't put his weight on the leg for long. He could hear water running over rock not far ahead. The path must have circled back towards the river. Ignoring the pain in his leg he doubled his effort to reach what he hoped was the Hawthorn tree.

A Wraith appeared at Tir's back its raptor claws slicing his leather vest like clay. Five shallow scratches opened up on Tir's back. His back arched as he spun swinging wildly. This time the dagger connected with the Wraith. It howled a hallow shrill and dissipated. Holding tight to the dagger Tir cleared the last few feet to the river bed. The forest held back leaving a semi-circle of low grass that gave way to reeds along the bank. Rising near the river bed the trunk of a Hawthorn crooked slightly over the river. White flowers bloomed across its branches. The only plant on this side of the forest. Tir spun leaving the tree to his right and the river to his back. He slowly stepped backwards looking for the flickering grey shapes.

One deep breath. Tir was exhausted. His leg throbbed. Two deep breaths. His hair clung to his sweaty and bloody covered back. Three. The first Wraith burst into the clearing clawed hands tearing at the air. As soon as it materialized in the semi-circle the transparency solidified. Tir dodged a slice and stabbed deep into the Wraith. It howled like the last one, but instead of disappearing this one shattered. Dark grey smoke fell to the ground and the howl died.

A cold wind hit Tir's naked chest. His heart ached with loneliness. He would be exiled. Aelsun had abandoned him. There was no hope. Tir took a deep breath relieving himself of the pity. It was sudden and fleeting lasting only as long as the cold wind on his skin. That frightened him. In an instant his entire self was altered. He didn't feel like himself in those moments. It was as if every part he thought good of himself left him somehow, leaving only the parts he dreaded to think about. The parts everyone has but refuse to acknowledge burying them deep under other feelings and memories.

Immediately, another Wraith shimmered into existence in front of him. Instincts took over and Tir shoved the blade into the Wraith's head, between the eyes. Another burst of cold wind seeped into Tir's chest. The depression lasted a heartbeat or two longer this time accompanied by a heaviness in his stomach. Two more Wraiths moved in on him and Tir wasn't sure he wanted to go through the feeling of killing these creatures again.

    He gripped the hilt tighter waiting for them to attack. The first swung at his chest while the other sliced at his neck. Tir held up his injured arm to block the attack at his neck. His skin contacted with a wet and cold arm as if the Wraith was made of ice. His clenched fist opened under the impact. The nerves jarred by the cold. He slammed the dagger home. Before the crippling depression dragged him down, he pulled the blade out and sliced across the second Wraith's chest. It cut across Tir's ribs with its claws as the dagger passed through it. Both Wraiths dissipated into grey clouds of vapor.

    Darkness encroached from the corners of Tir's eyes. The trees looked like enemies. Tir found it hard to track the Wraiths as they flickered from tree to shadow; edging their way towards him. Tir panted. Tears fell through the dirt covering his face. He should just let them kill him. He had no hope of surviving. How many were there? Ten more? Twenty? Aelsun might have known. Tir gripped the dagger in numbing fingers. If these were the feelings, he had to look forward too he wasn't sure he cared to live anymore. Five more Wraiths moved into the clearing before the depression had time to leave. While Tir thought of bliss in death a small portion of himself immune to depression ignited. Everything can change in a moment. When a person is pushed to the brink of death, a will to live can outshine almost anything. One of the Wraiths sliced Tir across the back nearly overlapping the previous cuts. Tir roared a battle cry. He flipped the blade over so that the tip faced the ground, then drove it behind him catching the Wraith in the side. The contact was enough to kill it. The others cut at him. One reopened the wound on his arm. Another stabbed him above the knee. A third cut deep lines across his chest, cutting through sweat, dried spit, and blood. Tir exacted their life as payment for their attacks. The blade flared brighter with each death. Tears ran from his eyes and his lipped quivered. His will to live kept the depression at bay.

Tir dropped to his knees in pain. His entire lower body contracted in muscle spasms. He cried a silent moan. Spittle spread between his lips. He couldn't believe he was still alive. It hurt to be alive. Each breath burnt as he inhaled. It felt like sharpened rocks as he exhaled. His hair hung in matted clumps. The band he used to hold it together lost in his dash and subsequent melee. The moving water came into focus behind him. He only now realized how thirsty he was. If it was cool water, he could fall into it and clean off his sticky skin. He rolled onto his stomach unwilling to stand. The cramping had subsided to a bearable ache and he didn't want to risk it returning. Thoughts of drowning came unbidden to his mind. His arms were exhausted but he wanted the water. He told himself one thing at a time. The pain would go away. If he could just get one thing in his life. Right now, he would be okay.

As he drew close, he could almost taste the crystalline water reflecting the moon light off slick rocks as it passed by. Frost spread over the water's surface. Thin sheets of ice broke off following the current away only to melt once passed the chilled air.

A single Wraith hovered over Tir. He flipped onto his back to stare into the hollow eyes of his death. He welcomed it. He welcomed a quick death. He would not get it. It wrapped its long twig like fingers around Tir's throat. Its touch was like smoldering fire wood. It didn't fear Tir. It ran a sharp nail from his collar down to his groin leaving blood in its wake. He had nothing left. Each time he killed one of them it took something from him. He wasn't sure what. Maybe life, a bit of his spirit, strength? He knew it was more than simply inflicting pain. The Wraith smiled down at him if it could be said to smile. Its featureless face blank of expression. Simply two empty sockets and a mouth stuck in a horrified scream. Not unlike some masks his people wore while dancing during festivals around large bon fires. The memory of those festivals usually brought a smile to his face. He felt nothing as he thought of his family, the mouth-watering food, laughter, competition. He was hollow. He knew the creature took pleasure in it.

He couldn't scream let alone breath as the Wraith dug its nail into his stomach piercing skin near his naval. Tir felt his insides get cut. Blood spilled over his stomach. The Wraith held his head so he couldn't see the damage. He felt the creature twist its nail in the wound. Tir groaned. His face turned into a grimace. The Wraith breathed deep, inhaling the pain Tir thought. It pulled the bloodied fingertip out of the wound and smeared the blood over Tir's lips. Tir coughed. Some of his blood caught in the back of his throat. The creature reared back. Tir saw through blurred vision. He desired death. Release from existence. He pleaded to Odin that it would come. It was a hollow plea. He felt miserable, but that spark he had ignited when he fought the half-dozen or so Wraiths hadn't died. As he wished to die, he also wished to live. The Wraith was readying for the killing blow he thought. Needle like nails raised to skewer his head to the ground. His last thoughts were of the cool water just out of reach. Then blackness.

***

Aelsun forced himself to focus. The Wraiths he managed to kill extracted their price. Tiny fragments of his soul were offered for each one he killed. His quiver held one arrow left. If there were more Wraith's than that well, he would get Tir out of here and face them somehow. It didn't matter. That boy was innocent. He was a simple child living a simple life. He didn't need to know of the things Aelsun dealt with out here. He didn't deserve a fate of sorrow and isolation. A small part of him hoped it would pay back a debt his people owed for their long isolation.

He came upon the clearing. Tir on his back and a Wraith atop him digging its claw into his stomach. The dagger lay midway between the elf and the human. Aelsun plucked the arrow from his quiver, raven feathers tickling his palm. He notched the arrow and drew back on his bow at the same time. He said a prayer to the arrow. He prayed it would fly true as all of his previous had this night. He held his breath and loosed. The glow tipped arrow pierced the air then the Wraith. Its empty howl hit Aelsun in his chest, but another piece of his spirit wasn't gone.

****

A deep breath found its way into Tir's lungs. The aches, stings, and pains were a welcomed feeling. He smelled the freshness of the forest around him. His tongue ached for the sweet clear water babbling behind him. He rolled onto his stomach and crawled the rest of the way unsure of why he had stopped. He dipped his hands in making a bowl out of them and drank from it. The crisp water broke over his tongue. He sighed. His pain vanished in that brief moment. He finished off several more handfuls of water then got to his feet.

"I've only seen a wolf drink more sloppily than that."

Tir spun to see Aelsun stepping from the surrounding woods swinging his bow over his back.

"I didn't think it needed to be said, but losing your weapon in battle could come with deadly consequences." Aelsun's humor was lost on Tir. He nodded and began to defend his actions. Aelsun held up his hand. "Rest up. You've done well. If you desire to make your home in time we need to move."

"Did we get them all?" Tir said sitting down in the cool water. The water turned black and then grey around him as the grime was carried away.

"All? No. But the pack that hunted you is dead. Any Wraiths you come across in the future will hunt you as veraciously as these. Regardless of what Ivelk infected you."

"Can I ask you a question?"

The elf raised an eye-brown expectantly.

"When I killed the Wraiths, it hurt me. Is that normal?"

"Yes. Every time you kill a Wraith, every time," Aelsun repeated himself eyeing Tir closely. For what reason Tir couldn't guess. "It hurts. A Wraith is a special creature not really of our world and not of the afterworld either. I'm not a scholar so I will tell you how I know it best. When you kill a Wraith, you force it out of our world. When you do, it takes a price from the one who killed it. The price represents itself in pain."

"I didn't think I could have killed another one. Each time I felt as if a cold wind hit me in the chest hard as any of my father's warriors. I'd hate to face anymore."

"Let's hope you don't have to. Now rest. We leave shortly."

Tir rested as best he could. The hard ground did little to help his wounded body. Aelsun tended to the wounds old and new before they left. It was midday when they struck out. Aelsun was confident Tir would make it to his village before dawn broke on the tenth day of his trial. Over the three days journey they faced little in the way of threats. At least compared to the Ivelk and Wraith. A bandit crossed their path and Tir was stunned by Aelsun's skill with a bow. He hadn't been able to appreciate the grace the elf used while being attacked by the Wraiths. Now a single bandit was laughable. Wolves could be heard the first night, but once the left the Sentient Wood the howling stopped. Perhaps the wolves turned away or perhaps the predator became prey. Tir tried not to think of that. By the third day his body hurt less and his wounds began to heal. They weren't far from Tir's village when Aelsun stopped for a brief respite. The elf's timeframe was a little optimistic. It would be late afternoon when Tir arrived at his village, still within a legal timeframe. He drew out the glowing dagger and handed it to Tir.

"I want you to have this Tir."

"You believe I'll need it?"

"I do." The gift was made from sorrow not delight. Aelsun didn't want to have to part with the blade. It was one of a few remaining in the world. He took it when he left his home. Its simple handle wrapped with brown leather held an iron alloy blade. He released it before he could change his mind. The boy would need it more than he. He repeated that over to himself.

"Thanks," Tir said. He was genuine and reluctant. Slipping the blade in his belt he turned in the direction of his village. "I guess we should get going."

"No. This is where I leave you. Your village is just passed the rise."

"Why part now? Why give me this?"

"I hope you never have to use it. I fear that is naïve however. Just take it a pray to your gods it is not needed. I think it would be best if your people did not know of me. My people's reputation is deserved and I find it easier to limit threats. You've seen the ones I already face. Adding humans only complicates my task more. Besides it makes you appear stronger to have survived this on your own does it not?"

"Any chance I could help you with your task?"

"You have been burdened enough for one lifetime I believe. Go live as best you can amongst your people. Do not worry on my task."

Tir nodded. He held out his hand for the elf and they grasped forearms. Neither said goodbye or exchanged further farewells. Their paths crossed and their journeys continued on separate trajectories. Aelsun leapt to the nearest tree and vanished. Tir walked the rest of the way to his village He stepped into the meadow he called home to be congratulated by all who knew him. He was a hero to them. To survive ten days outside and return with tales of wonder and awe had not been done in generations. His people heaped praise onto him. They held him up as if he were Thor himself. Tir couldn't focus enough to blush. His eyes were drawn outside where Aelsun was. The tinge of loneliness still haunted his feelings tainting his happiness as the elf said it would. He forced a smile for his family and friends, celebrating with them for the night. He would have the rest of his life to deal with the burden he carried.

THE END

Author's Note

Before I begin, I wanted to say I put a lot of thought into this author's note. I know most will finish the story and bypass this, but for those interested I want you to receive quality and not something I added for extra pages. This isn't included in the digital copy because if you spent the extra money to own a paperback, I think you deserve a little more.

Tir's Trial like all of my work has in the foundation a philosophical theory. I originally went to college for philosophy before turning my sights on creative writing, but found that the two actually work well with one another. So, I endeavor to marry my two loves into one creative outlet, storytelling. In truth, at the core of all learning disciplines is a nugget of philosophy. From the first mathematician who contemplated the connectivity of quantities to the sociologist who wondered about human beings, philosophy was its beginning.

Belonging is something I think many adolescents struggle with. We are taught our parents split their chromosomes and gave us the two split sections so that we could mold them into one being. The randomization of those chromosomes leaves us as not quite either parent. As an outcast from birth how are we to find belonging? Are we best suited to travel the path of either parent or should we strike out on our own and hope we make the right choices. For Tir he's forced to participate in the coming-of-age ceremony and if he fails, he will not belong at home. He will be thrust out, an outcast separated from the social group that has accepted him. His village is more than a group living together though. Any man could be uncle or brother and any woman aunt or sister. His entire life is in the tribe. For him, being exiled is the same as losing who he is. In the end all we have is who we are no matter what our chromosomes say.

What is belonging? Are we born with a desire to belong? Is belonging with family engraved like in the godfather or is it taught? I think we are born with a desire to belong, to find a place we are comfortable and can be ourselves. Who that is with I think we decide as we grow. Some may find that by making their own family and others may still be seeking for that place. Many books like my story touch upon this subject, but I believe my take brings new light on the meaning of belonging when you feel forces beyond your control are acting on you.

Tir struggles with belonging throughout the story. At first normal teenage issues with finding his place then later more severely when it is savagely ripped from him by the wraith. The next question becomes can we survive without belonging somewhere? It could be a lonely life or perhaps others in his situation may find like souls who give them a resemblance of belonging.

I thought it would be fun to play with this idea for my character. I was the outcast growing up and while I think I turned out okay, I wondered about those who had it rougher than I did. Of course, this is a fantastical setting with man eating plants and vampire elves, but in fiction we can all relate to the others plight whether separated by worlds or millions of years.

For Tir I don't know how he will overcome his troubles at the end of the story, that's all part of his life, that he will have to live. And while I do have larger plans for this world, I haven't written it yet. So, for now take away what you will from this story.

Enjoy the tale for what it is or pick up the undertone I left behind. Regardless remember fiction is meant to escape our struggles and give us a break from our lives.

Look for me

Twitter   @bull4499

My website
https://alfredmuller44.wixsite.com/alfred-muller-books

YouTube
https://www.youtube.com/channel/UCr34bUXzBhs2ZSiRKup3-fw

Amazon   Alfred Muller

Made in the USA
Monee, IL
17 October 2024